Byron Through The Seasons

. . . .

Byron Beł Hait'azį Łuk'é Háye Sine

A DENE-ENGLISH STORY BOOK
BY THE CHILDREN OF LA LOCHE AND FRIENDS

FIFTH HOUSE PUBLISHERS

Canadian Cataloguing in Publication Data
Byron through the seasons
Text in English and Chipewyan.
Added title in Chipewyan.
ISBN 1-895618-33-9 (pbk.)
1. Tinne Indians - Juvenile literature.
I. La Loche Library Board.
E99.T56B97 1990 j971'.00497 C90-097053-7

Design: Robert MacDonald, MediaClones Inc.

Printed in Hong Kong.

The publisher gratefully acknowledges the assistance
of the Saskatchewan Arts Board, Communications
Canada, and The Canada Council.

FIFTH HOUSE
1511-1800 4th Street S.W.
Calgary, Ontario
T2S 2S5

FOUR HUNDRED AUTHORS

This book was produced by the students and teachers of Ducharme Elementary School in La Loche, Saskatchewan, with assistance from local advisors and elders. Together we wrote the story, translated it, and worked on the pictures.

Our goal was to highlight some aspects of Dene culture that were vital in the past and are still important today. We wanted to show the continuity of a genuine and successful way of life, and emphasize culturally-significant events and attitudes.

To produce the book, over 400 students provided ideas for the story line and art samples for the illustrations. Two hundred letters went out to community families, asking for ideas and information with regard to story content. A dozen elders were consulted to provide accurate and culturally-correct information. A teacher committee of six worked on the project for two years.

Byron Through the Seasons is a story told by Grandfather Jonas and imagined by his grandson, Byron. The balloon diagram in each picture represents the symbolic journey taken by Byron as he listens to stories of what Dene life is like during the four seasons of the year.

We would like to thank the Northern Lights School Board and the Saskatchewan Mining Development Corporation for their financial support of this project.

Readers are encouraged to refer to the Supplementary Information in the back of the book, which provides background material for the dialogue and illustrations.

Byron listens to the teacher.
"Quiet, everyone. Byron's grandfather, Jonas,
is going to tell us a story about the seasons
in La Loche."
As Jonas speaks, Byron dreams ...

. . . .

Byron sɛkwi hóneɬten huriɬtth'a.
Horɛlyu dárogus.
Byron betáuné Jonas núhɛl hólni háʔa
tthįtélaztué hógha.
Betáuné Jonas yaɬti hú Byron náte.

Illustration:
Ritchie Lemaigre

Ritchie Lemaigre

2

"In the fall, at camp, we catch and prepare some of our own food.
We buy the rest at the Bay.
Long ago we went to the Bay only a few times a year for sugar, lard, flour, and tea."

. . . .

Hait'azį de nahi núhéni decenyaghe hotsį.
Honesí núheni náinik'é hotsį.
Thá hú yanessa náinik'é tah húto dįh húto nédeɬni iɬagne hháye k'e suga hu tɬes hu ɬes hu ledi nádághilni.

Illustration:
Ritchie Lemaigre

"At fall camp I catch and dry fish.
I have been doing this from the time
I was a boy like Byron.
Grandmother and the kids pick berries
and help with the fish.
If we are lucky, we get a moose."

. . . .

Hait'azį kóek'é ⅄ue heslu hel dasgan.
Byron beghesį cilikwiuaze heslin' hú hotsį
beghanásther.
Setsuné sekwi hel jie oneye hú ⅄ue sédyįlé.
Núhelsen horini de dinie ⅄eghánesthi nį.

Illustration:
Ritchie Lemaigre

Ritchie Lemaigre

4

"As it turns colder
we get ready for winter.
We put the boats away
before the lake freezes."

· ·

Edza hacha de háye ba t'asirede.
Ts'i senilyé deten hile tu.

Illustration:
Ritchie Lemaigre

"In winter my boys use ski-doos
to pull their toboggans.
I like to use my dogs."

5

. . . .

Haye de se cilikwiuaze ski-doo
dadóreɬʔá bescene tseralu.
Sets'i ɬį̀ dadótrɬʔá senighi.

Illustration:
Calvin Lemaigre
and Ritchie Lemaigre

6

"When the ice is thick I take Byron fishing.
We give our friends some of the catch, and
cook the rest for supper.
Fish with lard and flour tastes so good."

. . . .

Hotigh' deten de Byron jetheda kuste ha.
Náhi nuheset'éni ⅄ue beghá yilye ha.
⅄ue tⅩes hel de dé?aze thécome.

Illustration:
Neil Janvier

7

"This winter the girls will learn how to make moccasins out of moose hide.
They will sew on coloured beads in patterns.
In the old days my grandma made patterns on her moccasins with porcupine quills."

. . . .

Dųgháyek'ɛ Byron betsuné ts'ekwaze hadónelten dinie téth ʔa ké heltsį ha.
Įɫtsiuze ʔa yenéɫką.
Yanessa dene ts'ic'oghe ʔa ké dáyeɫtsį ni.

Illustration:
Dale Herman

8

"In late winter and early spring we cut ice blocks for the ice house, which keeps the fish cold in warm weather.
We have to do this before breakup."

. . . .

Haye honisé Ɫuk'etsen de ten hareɫdeth tenkóe ha.
Edu de Ɫue tenkóe bek'éghį̇lni.
Ten dete Tsen du korélye.

Illustration:
Calvin Lemaigre

CALVIN. LEMAIGRE

9

"In the spring we go to bush camp. There is lots of work to do but it feels good to be outside again."

. . . .

Łuke de decenyaghe tsen nahídel.
ʔasi la holeh kolú bit'azi násether horélya.

Illustration:
Gary Montgrand
and Michael Herman

GARY MONTGRAND

Michael Herman

10

"Nothing tastes as good as bannock cooked on an open fire."

....

Lést'eth ʔasi bɛ húlniʔle bit'azi thet'e de.

Illustration:
Ritchie Lemaigre

"At bush camp, before we tan the hides we kept over the winter, grandma scrapes them. Sometimes we help her."

11

· ·

Dechenya nade' hu edhéth
da'háye ghelá setune yełthi.
Nák'e setune betsendedi.

Illustration:
Neil Janvier

12

"When the strawberries are ripe
and it's time to plant the garden,
we pack up for summer camp."

. . . .

Įdziyaze néhler de nonesyeha
nelyé nuhnither de ʔasį dánaghégel
hú sine ha náhįdel.

Illustration:
Greg Janvier
and Bobby Guetre

Greg Janvier
BobbyGuet

"We work at summer camp but there is time for fun, too."

13

Sine eghédalaghida kolu są ha tthi hoʔa.

Illustration:
Ritchie Lemaigre

"While the little ones are swimming, grandma and the older kids pick special plants to make old-time medicine."

14

· ·

T'a dane cile tue nadé
Setuné sekwi hel anchą́ kadolʔe beʔah honis
hots'i náidii holeh ha.

Illustration:
Ritchie Lemaigre

15

"We leave summer camp in July
to go to Lac Ste. Anne to pray.
We visit with many people
from La Loche and other places.
It is a special time."

. . . .

Sine de ɛcedh zaghé k'é yati kédél.
Dene Ɂá hel kóɛta dethiltth'i.
Nani núhennán hotsį hu nani
ahsii ghé hotsį.

Illustration:
Ritchie Lemaigre

As Jonas ends his story and says goodbye,
Byron's thoughts return to the library.
"Thank-you, Jonas," he says.

16

. . . .

Setsié Jonas behoni belaghe hú Good-bye
heni.
Byron bịni erihtł'isk'oe tsen naghełé.
Marci setsie Jonas.

Illustration:
Ritchie Lemaigre

Ritchie Lemaig

Artwork Group

Top Left	Neil Janvier
Top Center	Calvin Lemaigre
Top Right	Ritchie Lemaigre
Middle Left	Gregory Janvier
Middle Right	Dale S. Herman
Bottom Left	Bobby Guetre
Bottom 2nd Left	Dale Laprise
Bottom 2nd Right	Donna Lee Dumont
Bottom Right	Rodney Janvier

Elders

Jonas Clarke
Philomene Fontaine
Arsene Fontaine
Raphael Janvier
Marie Lemaigre

Translators

Sally Lemaigre
Celina Janvier

Teacher Committee

Melva Schmidt
Wanda Rutten
Anne Frey
Trudy Henry
Sally Lemaigre
Gordon Rutten

Color Illustrator

Donna Lee Dumont

Supplementary Information

Story Background

The Following material has been prepared in order to provide a richer understanding of the Dene way of life as presented in the story and pictures of *Byron Through the Seasons*.

In the story, Grandfather Jonas talks about the seasons, recalling significant things and events in the daily life of the Dene people. Some of these have not changed much since people his age were young, but others have been adapted to modern times while still retaining their meaningfulness. In the sections that follow, the way things used to be is described, and modern changes are noted.

Income

In the old days, the people produced a lot of their own food, clothes, and other items, but they needed money to buy some things at the Bay. While camping out in family groups during the summer, they would make things that could be sold in the fall to pay for winter provisions. Men made birch-bark canoes and snowshoes, while women made baskets, moccasins, and leather mitts. At the end of the summer, these products were sold or traded to other people in the community or to the Bay.

Similarly, winter products were sold or traded in the spring. During the winter men hunted and trapped animals such as moose, bear, beaver, rabbit, squirrel, fox, ermine, otter, and lynx. Women prepared the meat and cleaned and tanned hides, both for personal use and for sale or trade.

In this way, two times a year a family's extra supplies were laid in — once in the spring from the proceeds of hunting and once in the fall from summer work.

The main items that were bought from the Bay were: sugar, tea, salt, flour, cloth, traps, guns, and bullets. Tea came in square tins cans of 2.25 and 4.5kg. Sugar cubes, butter, and jam came in rectangular wooden boxes of 4.5 to 6.75kg.

A typical family's fall food goal might include: two moose or one moose and one bear, 2000 fish, 45kg of flour, 9kg of tea, 4.5kg of salt, and 13.6kg of sugar.

Historically the Hudson's Bay Company bought furs, canoes, and leather items from the people and sold them basic food staples. To this day the Bay is located in almost every Northern community, and continues to buy furs and sell groceries and clothing.

Many Northern people still make mukluks, gauntlet mitts, and moccasins to sell. Often these items are beautifully beaded in soft, symmetrical designs which emphasize floral-based patterns. Commercial fishing continues to be a good source of income, and of course, many people have regular 9-to-5 jobs in the community.

Tanning

A long tradition of producing high-quality tanned hides continues unchanged over the decades. To tan a hide, a fire of old wood and moss is started in an old tub or a shallow hole in the ground. The hide is sewn together to form a round, tent-like shape, closed at the top. A strip of canvas is sewn to the bottom of the hide and staked to the ground or tied to the tub, so that the tent-like hide becomes a nearly air-tight enclosure over the fire. During two to five hours the heavy smoke saturates the hide to produce a deep fawn colour and the distinctive smoky scent of freshly-tanned leather.

Food Handling

Long ago, in the spring and summer any game that was killed was eaten quickly to avoid spoilage. In the fall, weather conditions were just right for preserving meat and fish by drying it. For this reason a great deal of hunting took place in the fall, and the meat was cut into thin strips and hung on poles to dry. At any season, all parts of hunted animals were used — brains for softening hides, fat for cooking and to burn for light, the heart and liver as delicacies, bones as scrapers, and marrow as a base for stew.

Today the hunting tradition continues to provide a supplement to regular groceries. Monday's supper might be roast beef and baked potatoes, with ice cream for dessert. Later in the evening the kids might have a cheeseburger and fries at the restaurant. Tuesday's supper might be rabbit stew, fried moose steak, or baked whitefish.

Drying fish is still done in two ways. The old way is to clean the fish and hang them up to dry by their tails with the heads left on, so that each fish is still in one piece. The new way is to remove the heads and tails and cut the fish into fillets before drying.

Often when flour was scarce it was extended with fish eggs, producing "caviar bannock." Even today fish eggs are eaten as a special treat, sometimes added to flour and sometimes deep-fried in a flour-based batter.

Bannock

Bannock is unleavened bread made from flour, water, baking powder, and lard. It can be baked in a pan, cooked over an open fire, wrapped around a small branch (bannock-on-a-stick), or deep-fried. It is often eaten fresh and hot with lard and jam.

Cooking

In the old days, cooking was done outside over open fires. Even today many older people prefer the taste of food cooked outside. Fat from the moose or bear — often referred to as "grease" — was used for cooking. To this day many foods are cooked in store-brought lard, which is also spread on fish and other meats as a taste-enhancer.

Preserving Food

Long ago, food was carefully preserved in a number of ways. Meat and fish were dried in the fall, and sometimes fat and berries were added to meat in order to cure it. Another common way of preserving food was to peel back layers of muskeg, dig a hole one metre deep, place the food inside, and re-cover the hole. Food was also kept in ice houses made from blocks of ice cut out of the frozen lake in the early spring. These ice houses were mainly used to preserve fish during the summer, and ice blocks are still used for this purpose today.

Berries and syrup

Berries were eaten fresh in the summer. In the fall they were picked to mix with dried meat and lard to form the well-known pemmican. Sometimes the berries were boiled in water to produce a thick, syrupy jam, which was stored for use in winter.

Birch trees were tapped in the spring for syrup, which was eaten in winter along with dried meat and fish.

Today people still go berry-picking, but birch trees are no longer plentiful enough or large enough to produce much syrup, although each spring a few people tap the best trees for a special treat.

A feast

Long ago in order to bring in the new year, many families would hold a feast that lasted all day and all night. Friends and family were invited. Outside fires were lit, and huge pots were set up to cook moose meat, bear meat, and rabbit. Several sacks of flour were turned into bannock; boxes of sugar were added to litres of tea. Entertainment included drum music, square dancing, games of checkers, fiddle playing, and tunes on the mouth organ.

Today New Year's Eve is a big event and many family gatherings are held. At midnight people go outside and fire guns into the air and set off fireworks.

Medicine and health

In the old days, medicine came directly from nature. The leaves of young birch or poplar were placed over serious wounds to prevent infection and speed healing. Many plants were used to make medicinal drinks. The roots of the cattail and the bark of the tamarack tree were boiled to produce a treatment for coughs and the flu. Rosehip tea was good for an upset stomach. The Labrador Tea plant was boiled to make a drink for reducing high blood pressure. To cure mouth infections the tops of pine cones were boiled to form a dark, syrupy drink.

A doctor flew into the community only once a month, but nuns often had nursing backgrounds, and local midwives delivered most of the babies.

Today the health needs of the people are attended to at a modern hospital and a community clinic. On occasion, though, the old medicines are used, and Native healers are consulted. Rosehip tea is still used regularly to settle an upset stomach.

Soap

Soap was made from the fat of the bear, caribou, or moose, with lye or wood ash added to it. The mixture was boiled thoroughly, cooled, and cut into squares.

Houses

Houses, in the old days, were made of logs, with moss serving as insulation between the logs. The roof was made of small trees covered with a layer of clay and topped with overlapping layers of meadow grass.

The windows were covered with the scraped skin of the mariah fish, which was translucent and let in a good deal of light.

Heat was provided by a fire in a fireplace made of rocks and clay. Iron and copper pots hung over the fireplace. Rabbits and large cuts of moose were hung and roasted there.

Light was provided by the fire and by kerosene lamps or home-made lamps which burned animal fat in a tin can with a strip of cotton for a wick.

Beds had log frames with mattresses of canvas or moose hide filled with moose hair or duck feathers.

Today, of course, houses are as modern as any found in the towns of Saskatchewan. A few people still maintain old-style log homes in the bush near their traplines.

Tobacco

When there was no money for tobacco from the Bay, people would crumble birch leaves and smoke them in pipes made by carving a small bowl in a rosehip tea bud, poking a hole in the side with a sharp stick, and inserting a green straw for a stem.

The camp circuit

Years ago families had one log house which served as a winter home, and in the other seasons they lived in a tent. In April they went to spring camp. People moved from 15 to 50 km, depending upon the availability of game. Transportation was by horse, by foot, and by pack dog. There were usually friends and relatives at these camps. A second move to summer camp took place in July to follow new game and meet different friends. A third move would occur in the fall — to a good fishing lake and a good berry supply. The families moved back into their log homes in early winter.

Today some of the people still go to camp, usually for periods of two to four weeks at different times of the year. Transportation is by half-ton truck and three-wheeler.